Little Grey Rabbit's Pancake Day

The Little Grey Rabbit Library

Little Grey Rabbit's Pancake Day

Alison Uttley

pictures by Margaret Tempest

Collins

William Collins Sons & Co Ltd
London · Glasgow · Sydney · Auckland
Toronto · Johannesburg

First published 1967
© text The Alison Uttley Literary Property Trust 1988
© illustrations The Estate of Margaret Tempest 1988
© this arrangement William Collins Sons & Co Ltd 1988
Fourth impression 1989
Cover decoration by Fiona Owen
Decorated capital by Mary Cooper
Alison Utteley's original story has been abridged for this book.
Uttley, Alison
Little Grey Rabbit's Pancake Day.–
Rev. ed – (Little Grey Rabbit books)
I. Title   II. Tempest, Margaret
III. Series
823'.912[J]   PZ7

ISBN 0-00-194223-9

Typeset by Columns of Reading
Made and Printed in Great Britain by
William Collins Sons and Co Ltd, Glasgow

FOREWORD

Of course you must understand that Grey Rabbit's home had no electric light or gas, and even the candles were made from pith of rushes dipped in wax from the wild bees' nests, which Squirrel found. Water there was in plenty, but it did not come from a tap. It flowed from a spring outside, which rose up from the ground and went to a brook. Grey Rabbit cooked on a fire, but it was a wood fire, there was no coal in that part of the country. Tea did not come from India, but from a little herb known very well to country people, who once dried it and used it in their cottage homes. Bread was baked from wheat ears, ground fine, and Hare and Grey Rabbit gleaned in the cornfields to get the wheat.

The doormats were plaited rushes, like country-made mats, and cushions were stuffed with wool gathered from the hedges where sheep pushed through the thorns. As for the looking-glass, Grey Rabbit found the glass, dropped from a lady's handbag, and Mole made a frame for it. Usually the animals gazed at themselves in the still pools as so many country children have done. The country ways of Grey Rabbit were the country ways known to the author.

ne day Hare was rummaging about in the bottom of the hedge, looking for what he could find, when he found something. It was an old frying-pan, very small, made of copper, but it was worn so thin it had been thrown away.

Hare rubbed it with a pad of grass dipped in sand, and he scrubbed it with a pad of grass dipped in water, and he polished it with a bunch of prickly furze, until it shone like gold. He filled it with water but the water ran out through a hole.

"Moldy Warp can mend this hole," said Hare. "He is good at making things. He can mend. I'll ask him to mend this."

Hare carried the little pan to Mole's house. Mole was digging in the garden, making a tunnel.

"Hello, Hare!" said he, putting down his spade. "What's that you've got?"

"A gold pan," said Hare, showing his treasure.

The Mole took it and examined it.

"It's not gold, it's pure copper," said Mole. "I can easily mend it. It's a frying-pan for eggs." He put a little clay into the hole, and sealed it up with some ironstone so that it was as good as new.

"We'll get some eggs from the Speckledy Hen," cried Hare. "I will take it home to Grey Rabbit."

He danced off, waving the little frying-pan, and banging it on the gorse bushes and on the hedges, to hear its music.

Grey Rabbit was delighted. "It's a pancake pan," said she, touching the copper with her soft paw and looking at her reflection in the metal.

"It's a looking-glass pan," said Squirrel, and she leaned over and tied her crooked ribbon neatly.

"It's a frying-pan for eggs. Mole told me," said Hare crossly.

"Yes," said Grey Rabbit calmly. "It's useful for many things – eggs and pancakes. When it isn't making pancakes we can look at ourselves."

"I shall make a banjo out of it," said Hare suddenly. "But tell us about pancakes, Grey Rabbit."

"It's Pancake Day next week," said Grey Rabbit. "We will give a party and invite Fuzzypeg and make pancakes."

Squirrel and Hare could hardly wait. They asked the Speckledy Hen to bring as many eggs as she could carry. They wrote a little letter to Fuzzypeg.

Robin the postman took the holly-leaf letter to Fuzzypeg's house. It had three words on it, and Robin popped it into Mrs Hedgehog's letter-box.

"Pancake Day. Come," it said. Fuzzypeg could read easily and he was delighted to get a letter.

"Mother, what is Pancake Day?" he asked.

"It's the day people eat pancakes," said Mrs Hedgehog, and Mr Hedgehog added, "Pancakes for hungry folk, very good feeding. It's many a day since I tasted a pancake, wife, not since I found one tossed out of a house right on to the common."

"I've never had one," said little Fuzzypeg.

"Well, we never have any eggs for pancakes," said Mrs Hedgehog, "but Grey Rabbit has the Speckledy Hen for a friend, so she can make pancakes."

She put little Fuzzypeg into a clean blue smock, and brushed his paws clean. "You go when the church clock strikes twelve," said she.

Fuzzypeg sat on a green bank near the door and listened for the church clock. There were no dandelion clocks to tell the time and nobody had a watch except Hare. Mr Hedgehog had planted a stick near the door, to tell the time by the shadow on the ground. Fuzzypeg watched the shadow getting shorter, but time moved slowly and he played a game with five stones which he tossed into a hole.

Then Mrs Hedgehog gave him a cup of milk.

"Drink this, Fuzzypeg," said she kindly. "It's cold out there on the bank looking at Time."

"I'm all right, Mother," said the small hedgehog, and another hedgehog joined him and played with him.

At last the shadow was very short, and the church clock struck twelve. Fuzzypeg ran indoors and kissed his mother. "Goodbye, Mother. I'm off to Grey Rabbit's house."

The church bells began to ring to warn people to make their pancakes.

"It's Pancake Day," they sang.

As Fuzzypeg trotted along the narrow track in the field he saw the ground heave, and out came Mole's head.

"Hello, Fuzzypeg," said Moldy Warp. "Where are you going so fast?"

"To Grey Rabbit's because it's Pancake Day," said Fuzzypeg.

"Well I never! I had quite forgotten about pancakes," muttered Mole, and he scrambled out of the hole, shook the dirt off his waistcoat and went along by Fuzzypeg's side.

"I shall go too," said he. "It's many a day since I had a taste of pancake. Not since one was tossed out of a doorway on the common. I think Grey Rabbit is going to use the pan I mended for her," said Mole, smacking his lips.

So away they went, walking fast to get to Grey Rabbit's house.

"Hist!" cried Mole. "There's the Fox. Let's go down through that gorse bush archway. It's safer."

Too late! The Fox had spied them.

"Where are you two off to in the middle of the day?" said he, smiling a big wide smile.

"To Grey Rabbit's house. It's Pancake Day," called Fuzzypeg.

"Pancake Day! Well! Well! I should like a taste of pancake. Never had one since I found a hen's nest with six eggs, and I made a pancake myself. Ah, that was a day. I'll go with you," said he, and he hopped behind them, making the Mole shiver, but Fuzzypeg stuck out all his spikes and didn't care.

"Can't take a fox to Grey Rabbit's house," whispered the Mole. "She won't like it, and Mr Hare will be very cross."

"Oh, Mr Fox," said Fuzzypeg sweetly, "if you will wait outside the garden wall I will toss a pancake to you."

"Thank you, Fuzzypeg," said the Fox. "It would be easier for all of us." So he dropped behind and the two hurried on to warn Grey Rabbit.

As they went up the garden path the door
was suddenly flung open and out flew the
Speckledy Hen.

"Oh dear!" she squawked. "My eggs are all
squashed."

"What's the matter, Speckledy Hen?"
asked Mole kindly, as he tried to soothe the
ruffled Hen.

"Hare s-s-sat on my nice eggs,"
cried the Hen. "I am going home. I
am annoyed and affronted."

"Mind the Fox," cried Fuzzypeg as the Hen flew over the gate. She squawked again as she rose up and flew over the Fox's head. Away they went, the poor Hen flying and the Fox leaping up to grab her. He got her bonnet, that was all, and he lay down with it between his paws.

"My wife will like this," said he. Grey Rabbit and Squirrel welcomed Mole and Fuzzypeg. "Poor Speckledy Hen! Come in and sit down."

"Hare sat on the eggs!" giggled Squirrel.

"I scooped them into a bowl. None the worse." said Hare.

"There are egg-shells sticking to your coat," said Squirrel.

"I like egg-shells in my coat," said Hare.

Fuzzypeg laughed. "Funny old Hare," he thought. He picked up the frying-pan and looked at himself.

"Oh, Grey Rabbit, I can see my blue smock and my prickles better than in the stream," said he.

"It's for making pancakes," explained Grey Rabbit. "I shall cook them in that pan." She turned to Mole. "Thank you, dear Moldy Warp, for making it shine and mending it."

"Thank you, dear Hare, for finding it," added Hare crossly.

"Yes," laughed Grey Rabbit. "Thank you for breaking the eggs."

She beat the eggs and some milk in the flour with a brush made of birch twigs till they frothed. She put the frying-pan over the fire with a little butter in it, and poured in some of the mixture. She sprinkled a few drops of sorrel juice squeezed from the wild wood-sorrel leaves, to give a sourness to the pancakes. The mixture ran all over the pan, bubbling and spreading out.

Everybody watched the clever rabbit, who raised the edges of the pancake with a thin little stick. Then with a sudden jerk of her paw, she tossed the pancake up in the air and caught it in the pan the other side up.

"Hurrah!" they cried. "Hurrah! She's caught it!"

"Not quite ready," warned Grey Rabbit, excited with her work. She fried the other side of the pancake and then she turned to her friends.

"Now, I shall toss it again and whoever catches it can have it."

She ran out of doors with the frying-pan and the pancake, and they all ran after her. She threw the golden pancake high in the air and waited. All the little animals leapt up to catch it, but Hare leapt the highest and he grabbed it, and wrapped it on his head like a hat.

"Oh it's hot!" said Hare.

"Eat it!" cried Grey Rabbit. "It isn't a hat. Eat it before it gets cold."

So Hare gobbled it up, muttering, "Delicious!"

"Let me make the next, Grey Rabbit," he begged.

So he held the pan over the fire, and then he gave a strong whisk at the batter which was ready in the bowl.

He ran outside to toss the pancake and everyone ran after him.

He tossed so hard the pancake went over the hedge into the field. The Fox caught it and ran swiftly to a sheltered spot to eat it.

"Better than my usual supper," he muttered, "but I will wait to see if any more come my way."

Squirrel begged Grey Rabbit to give her the next turn. "I'm a good cook, Grey Rabbit," she said, smiling as she took the frying-pan. She wiped it with a bit of leafy rag and poured in the batter. She held the pan over the fire while everyone gave advice.

"Don't throw too hard!" cried Fuzzypeg in a squeak.

"Don't put your tail in it," added Hare.

"Don't let the Fox get it," warned Grey Rabbit.

Squirrel smiled again. She tossed the pancake and caught it, she cooked the other side gently till the pancake was light as a feather.

She ran out of doors with it and tossed it
gently in the air. A breeze caught it as if it
were a bird and it fluttered high above the
trees. "Oh! Oh! Oh!" they cried as they
watched it.

Wise Owl had come to see what was the noise. When he saw the yellow pancake floating in the tree-tops, he swooped and caught it, and carried it home.

"It's a pancake, a real live pancake," he hooted, as he ate the delicious morsel, then he went back to bed murmuring,

"Too whit. Too whoo.
A pancake or two,
Or three or four,
If they fly to my door."

Back at the little house Moldy Warp was busy making a little pancake for himself. He put an extra egg in it, which he had found, and a pinch of honey and a sprinkle of wild thyme.

He made a neat little pancake and carried it quietly to the door. He waited till all was quiet.

"One to be ready.
Two to be steady.
Three to be OFF,"

he chanted, and he tossed the pancake only a few inches up in the air and caught it in the pan.

Then he sat down and ate it, but he gave a piece to poor Squirrel.

Fuzzypeg made a pancake. He tossed it only a short distance and he caught it on his spikes. So he had to turn his head to eat it.

It was so sweet, so crinkly and crisp, that Fuzzypeg thought it was the nicest food he had ever tasted.

"I tossed it, I tossed it," sang Fuzzypeg, and he ran back to the house.

Then Grey Rabbit made the last pancake with the last scrap of egg and the last scraping of flour. It was a very small pancake and she divided it between Fuzzypeg and herself.

As she ate it she sang a little song to the others who were scrubbing the copper frying-pan with bunches of grass, and tidying the house.

This is her song:

"Pancake Day! Pancake Day!
Fuzzy and Mole have come to play.
Grey Rabbit will toss it
And Hare will Eat it.
And Squirrel will catch it on Pancake
Day."

"Pancake Day! Pancake Day!
A pancake for Squirrel,
A pancake for Mole,
A snippet for Rabbit
Down in a hole,
A piece for the Owl
Up in the tree,
And a very small pancake for Fuzpeg and
me."

Then Hare fetched a piece of wire from the fence in the field, and Mole stretched it across the frying-pan to make strings. He tightened them with his strong paws, and made a tiny bridge of wood across the centre of the frying-pan. The wires were soon fastened across the frying-pan's middle, and Hare took the musical frying-pan in his paws. He pulled the strings and made a little singing sound like the wailing of the wind.

"It's a singing frying-pan," said he. "A banjo," said Mole. So Hare twanged it and Grey Rabbit sang until the stars came out in the sky and the Fox came out of his den, and the Owl flew out of his tree.

"I can hear a fearful tune," hooted Wise Owl. "I can hear a caterwauling at Grey Rabbit's house. I wonder what it is?" He flew over to look and he saw all the animals sitting at the door singing, "Pancake Day! Pancake Day!"

"That's the worst song I ever heard," he hooted.

But Grey Rabbit took off the wires and made the banjo into a frying-pan again. The next day Speckledy Hen brought some more eggs and they had another feast, and Wise Owl did not get a share.